The Little Yellow Truck

by Judy Hindley
Pictures by John Richardson

Collins Colour Cubs

Shiny little yellow truck,
Ready for a ride,

Packed up, doors shut,
I wonder what's inside?

Is it milk? Or coal?
Or apples?
Is it pigs or cows?

Is it ice-cream? Is it logs?
Is someone moving house?

Is it parcels?
No, it can't be,
Here's a parcel van.

Is it eggs and crates of milk?
No! *Here's* the milkman.

And here's a truck for cattle
And it isn't one of those.

And here's a dairy tanker
Getting filled up with a hose,
And it isn't one of those.

So what's inside the yellow truck?
Let's see where it goes.

Past a car transporter
Giving brand-new cars a ride.

Past a big pantechnicon
With furniture inside.

Past a truck with racks of clothes,
Skirts and shirts and jeans.

A truck with coal,

A truck with fruit,

A van that sells ice-creams.
But what's inside the yellow truck?
Whatever can it be?
Hey! I think it's slowing down.
Perhaps we're going to see.

Stop the engine!
Set the brake!
Throw the back doors wide!

Carry in the boxes,
What is this inside?
Look —

TINY
Little yellow trucks

Ready for a ride!